FAMILIES AMONG US

FAMILIES AMONG US
STORIES
BLAKE KIMZEY

Black
Lawrence
Press

Black
Lawrence
Press

www.blacklawrence.com

Executive Editor: Diane Goettel
Chapbook Editor: Kit Frick
Book design: Amy Freels
Cover design: Angela Leroux-Lindsey
Cover art: *Free Soil Thirty-One* by Pat Perry. Used with permission.

Published 2014 by Black Lawrence Press.
Printed in the United States.

ACKNOWLEDGMENTS
Grateful acknowledgement is made to the following magazines,
where these stories first appeared:

Dark Sky Magazine (and adapted for broadcast on NPR): "A Family Among Us"
PANK: "Up and Away"
Structo (England): "The Skylight"
Her Royal Majesty (France): "Tunneling"
Tin House: "And Finally the Tragedy"
The Masters Review: "The Boy and The Bear"

For Danielle and June

More Praise for *Families Among Us*

In these six controlled and full-hearted tales, Blake Kimzey propels his characters into a wilderness that threatens and promises to obliterate our old notions of home. Steeped in legend and grounded by nature, *Families Among Us* is a powerful reminder that one can, even in the most supportive families, metamorphose into an adult whose only option is flight. What a terrific start to a long and bright career.
—Gabe Durham, author of *Fun Camp*

Kimzey brings us into the world we glimpsed with Kafka, where, with both clarity and mystery, we must confront the monster as family and the family as monster, the sorrow of separation as the liberation of leaving. This is what fiction is for.
—Josh Woods, editor of the *Surreal South '13* anthology

Blake Kimzey writes with enormous talent, imagination, and depth of feeling. The eerie, haunting fables that comprise *Families Among Us* are like dreams that bind abandonment and solitude to growth in a tragic and moving way, bearing out what Heraclitus said: "Nothing endures but change."
—Austin Ratner, author of the novels *In the Land of the Living* and *The Jump Artist*

Blake Kimzey's *Families Among Us* is a strong and stunning collection. The prose feels new, always imaginative and surprising, striking a beautiful balance of realistic and surreal. The stories—even when completely fantastical and lightly allegorical—always remain utterly human, and it's a powerful book that builds to something complete and wonderfully memorable.
—Harriet Alida Lye, editor of *Her Royal Majesty*

Contents

A Family Among Us

Four of them, a family, crawled naked from the sea clutching plastic suitcases. Like a brass section in an orchestra they drew breath into their lungs for the first time in days, months, years, decades. They were ageless, the mother and father, boy and girl. Slowly, the gills on their necks flattened and disappeared into skin, leaving only faint watermarks that suggested long forgotten scars or birthmarks. It hurt at first, their lungs rising and falling, rising and falling.

The decision to leave the sea was permanent, a unanimous vote to abandon the fuselage that had been their home, for how many years they could not count. On shore, among the smooth rocks and wet driftwood, they dressed. They stood on uncertain legs. Out of the water their arms seemed to move too fast, cutting through the air without resistance. For the first time the children heard waves crashing, birds overhead, and felt the warmth of the sun on their bare skin. A multitude of smells swirled about the children, and they smiled and dripped dry for the first time in memory.

The mother helped her daughter fasten a training bra and select a matching outfit from her suitcase. The father showed his boy how

to button a shirt, how to be precise with his small hands and fingers
so that he could make bunny ears with the shoelaces. Their clothes
came from the 1970s and suggested disco, roller skates, horizontal
stripes, primary colors, and brown corduroy. They had been underwater for some time, and emerged like lost luggage from a downed
PAN-AM flight.

It was days, maybe weeks, before they spoke. They stayed in the
forest, close to the shoreline. They returned to the water for food,
and took turns gathering wood a short distance from camp. At
night they huddled by a fire where they taught themselves coor-
dination, and dredged their minds for language, parts of speech,
agreement. The father cleared his voice over and over, as if to ease
his chords into waking life. The mother started to hum, suggesting
a beautiful voice, light and airy. For years they had been underwater,
using only eye movement and waterlogged faces to suggest emotion
or directions. The family had created shorthand in the fluid world
of the sea and was trying to begin anew on land.

Nightfall was easier on the eyes and soothing to their souls. The
murkiness of the woods at night made them feel at home. Muted
sounds, animals crying in the distance comforted them. Sunrise
was startling, a brutal start to each morning. The clarity of daytime
was difficult to comprehend, and the waking hours meant work of
all kinds, collective re-schooling on everything they had left behind
when they fell from the air those many years ago into the sea.

This new life wasn't as easy as the father and mother thought it
would be. The boy had nightmares, and would scream in his sleep,
scared of arboreal silhouettes and their vertical push skyward.
Gravity provided no comfort, and weighed on them all. The daughter was the first to refuse her clothes. First her bra, then her pants,
and within the week she was naked and running from the woods to
the water as soon as she was allowed. She refused to speak, and used

only her eyes to communicate. The boy followed suit. The water was fun, effortless, and before long he too was naked, emerging from the water reluctantly at the end of the day with pruned pale skin. But the children could no longer dive deep enough, or stay under water long enough, and returned to the surface gulping for air. Their heads were dizzy and bodies fatigued from fighting the water. They fought their lungs to the point of exhaustion. Every day the children made it their goal to stay under water for longer than they had the previous day. The boy and girl held on to each other so they could sink lower, where the water was dark, and still they would have to scramble to the surface in a panic for air. In time the girl could stay under water for eight minutes, the boy for five, and together they thought eventually they would be able to hold their breath forever.

The mother and father didn't know what to do. They were now able to talk about things, but the words came slowly. Those many months ago when they retrieved their suitcases from long forgotten compartments, and swam nervously to the surface, to shore, they never envisioned this. They were made for dry land, made for the openness of the countryside and the buzz of cities and cafes. By now they should have made their way into a city, where the transition would continue. They had so many dreams for the children.

And then, one night, the children didn't return to camp. The father called for them; his strengthening voice carried through the woods and came back in an echo. He and his wife walked a well-worn path to the seashore. The light was just fading and the surface of the water seemed to ripple into an unending horizon. The sun was hanging low, and then it was gone.

Dusk remained. The father had to squint, but he was the first to see them. He let out a scream as loud and strong as any in his lifetime. His wife buried her head in his chest and started to whimper, light and airy. The boy and girl were floating on the surface of the water, not ten yards away. Their pale naked bodies bobbed in the water, their arms tangled together, as if one form. The water became dark and the night sky was black and cloudless.

The father swam to the boy and the girl. He returned their bodies to shore. For hours the mother kneeled beside them and hugged them and cried over them. When she was done, the father carried the boy and girl into the woods and buried them in the soft earth at the base of the tallest tree in the forest.

When the father returned to the shore his wife was naked. Her clothes were gathered about her feet, and she glanced toward the sea. She again began to whimper. They held each other until the moon was high overhead. Without a word the father removed his clothes, one article at a time. Together they entered the sea, and swam until their lungs burned, and within the hour their heads bobbed out of sight. Where they went under only a slight ripple remained. They held on to each other, and sunk deeper and deeper, until everything was dark and their thoughts of land were no more.

Up and Away

The boy never made the cover of the black and white tabloids at the supermarket even though he learned to fly before he hit puberty. The curve in his back was subtle, but it was there and microfiche suggests he was born with a partial exoskeleton, what entomologists on record referred to as a beetle back. At the time there was some debate about his usefulness to science and if he should be studied. An unclassified government CD-ROM from 1987 documents his existence and suggests he might be of some use to the military, but there is no official mention of him after 1988.

The boy did disappear, but not immediately after 1988. There are yearbook photos from his time in elementary school, the headgear and braces and the over-gelled side-spike haircut forever immortalized after his parents moved from Chicago to the skinny part of Idaho near the mouth of the Snake River, where they thought they wouldn't be bothered. The boy grew like a regular boy, his voice cracked and he back-talked his mother, though each successive year his back curved more noticeably and his wings became stronger and his appetite larger. His mother thought the curvature of his beetle back was beautiful, the dark, waxy ridges in his skin and the seam running down the middle where human indentions of vertebrae were absent. She asked God how the boy had come from her womb, and wondered to what end could God allow the boy's existence?

The mother cherished the boy and thought him a blessing, a light in the family. Polaroids exist showing the beautiful black dots, like those on a Lady Bug, just under the wavy, indented skin below his shoulders. By third grade it looked like the boy was wearing a turtle shell under his shirts, and the boy's sister couldn't decide if his form was enhanced or mutated or deformed. The boy's sister never tired of staring at the deformity in the same manner as strangers and small children, who gawked openly. She would pat him on his back, tell him good job and hug him for no reason if only to feel the beetle back, to understand it, to touch it, to try and grasp the absurdity of nature. The boy ripped many shirts from uncontrolled spasms and injured his wings when there was no place for them to unfold. It was a hazard until he learned control. The boy walked in a hunched stance and tried to make up for it with good posture. His mother told a family friend that the boy slept on his stomach because sleeping on his back made him feel like a marooned crustacean.

Flying didn't come naturally for the boy. His father said in passing that it took the boy a year to control his beetle back, to regulate when his wings would come out. The exoskeleton had different wiring and the boy struggled to control two bodies at once. At first the boy could only flutter in the air for a moment, like an early pioneer of the jetpack rising unevenly in the inventor's backyard. Grainy home movies show the boy's back separating and translucent wings emerging; off-camera someone admires their beauty, the intermittent control, the flight. In slow motion the wings move rapidly and create a whirr of wind that the boy's father later joked was powerful enough to unhinge his combover.

For years the boy was unsteady in flight and his mother urged him to stay out of the air. The boy's sister remembered that if he started to hover in the living room their mother would become hysterical, worried about her glass figurines. There were tchotchkes in every corner of the house and an arrangement of antique wooden dolls stacked like produce on a table in the dining room. The boy's father collected tiny pewter soldiers, all of them staged on various shelves, looking up to defend a swarm of equally tiny, fire-breathing dragons suspended from the ceiling by fishing wire.

But the boy never broke any of the collectables. He learned to harness his form, and it wasn't long before he was gone for hours and then days at a time as his wings could carry him farther and farther. Mostly he flew north toward the Canadian border and beyond into the wilds of the Northern Forest where he could sate his appetite for earthworms, snails, animal dung, leaves, and all of the decomposed matter that winter left in its wake. Every time he left the boy said he would return. The time between his trips grew shorter and the boy had fewer things to say when he returned. Eventually the boy was silent, focused in a way no one in his family had seen before.

It was a clear evening the last time they saw the boy. He circled their house slowly and took off the last bits of his clothing. His Nikes and jean shorts came to rest on the roof, caught in the grit and stickiness of the shingles. Naked, the boy darted up and away and his family followed him until he was a dot in the sky, the way a helium balloon rises and then fades into the expanse. The boy's sister and his mother and his father stood on the lawn waving after him, calling for him to return. Days, weeks, months later the boy's mother fell ill and his father took to his work and his sister wrote and wrote and wrote about him, sometimes repeating the same sentences over and over again in her journal until there was nothing more she could say.

The Skylight

He liked that he was the only American in the building. Most of his neighbors were from North Africa. They owned the luggage shops and beauty salons lining the narrow street below. Some donned the bright green reflective jumpsuits of sanitation workers as they swept through the city and its parks day after day. One large man worked security at the Monoprix across the street, making sure kids didn't steal bags of Haribo gummies or plastic yogurt cups. It was an affordable neighborhood in the hills near Sacre Coeur that smelled of cumin and turmeric, and he could easily pay rent working as an English-speaking tour guide.

Something interested him about this part of the city when he was looking for an apartment four months ago. Large owls made their nests atop the buildings throughout the 18th arrondissement, perched like stone gargoyles at night; they reminded him of the watchful barn owls he knew from his home in rural Iowa. He marveled at the growing African diaspora in this part of Paris, and felt a kinship with them. Together, they were all foreigners in this city. The neighborhood mosque on *rue des Poissonniers* spilled into the street at the call to prayer, a cluster of intricate patterned mats arranged in rectangles across the pavement. The women in their hijabs and burqas, all of the men wearing a customary fez. There was nothing like it back home. At the tabac on the corner, men stood at the bar smoking cigarettes to the nub and sipped strong espresso from tiny ceramic cups. He would go there every morning, his foot propped on the low brass railing, and drink café au lait and listen to the swirl of French and Arabic that filled the small room. He towered over the men and looked out of place in his t-shirt and shorts, his faded baseball cap, his blue eyes, and the tip of his nose sunburned from working outside all day. Sometimes he saw his neighbor from the sixth floor at the tabac, an older man with a thin black combover, bags under his eyes, and a scar on the side of his neck from what looked like a small claw.

*

It had been a long day. He led 25 people out to Versailles on a bicycle tour that was a disaster. He had to change three flat tires at the end of the Grand Canal under a misting, overcast green sky. The scheduled picnic along the stone-lined canal was ruined, and his tour had to huddle under manicured poplar trees and eat quickly in cheap plastic parkas. It took forever to get through the Château, the stale hallways choked with perspiring tourists elbowing one another out of the way, all of them craning their necks from side to side in the Hall of Mirrors. His group missed the early RER back to Paris, which put everyone in a worse mood. Afterward, all the tour guides cycled to a Canadian bar in the Latin Quarter where the bartenders knew him and only made him pay for every other drink. Nearing 30 years of age, he didn't have a master plan, not after his engagement was called off, the wedding in Dubuque canceled. He let his fiancée go without a fight, off to Nebraska with another man. And now he was happy, a year later, to hide out at night and practice his bad French with Parisian women who would never go home with him.

He normally got home after midnight. He punched the door code and pushed through the big black double doors into the dark courtyard, and walked quietly with his bike toward the opposite stairwell. His apartment building didn't have an elevator, but few of the older ones in Paris did. He could still access the roof when he wanted. On the sixth floor a metal maintenance ladder led to a narrow skylight at the top of the stairwell. It took some effort to get on the centuries-old roof, soft in spots, with thin tin chimneys, tarpaper, and old television antennas that were bent from years of wind and rain. This is what he loved most about the building. From up there he could see the tip of the Eiffel Tower and across the expansive city to La Defénse. Normally he was the only one up there, keeping the owls company, feeding them bits of raw duck he purchased from the *boucherie*.

In the stairwell he flipped a switch and dim light bloomed from somewhere high above. He had his bike on his shoulder as he worked his way up the winding staircase to his apartment on the fifth floor. The entire building was like a library, eerily quiet from floor to floor. A young woman he had seen before, but never up close, climbed a few steps in front of him. He slowed so he wouldn't overtake her. He could never tell exactly how old she was because she was covered from head to toe, a mysterious mesh screen on her face-veil the only identifying marker. She seemed to glide up the steps as if she were weightless. The hem of her ankle-length burqa swept the steps as she climbed. She was ascending the corkscrew stairs toward the top floor, where she lived with her father, the man he sometimes saw at the tabac.

He stopped at his door on the landing of the fifth floor. He set his bike down and found his keys. Before entering his apartment he looked up at the young woman. She kept walking up the steps, but her head was turned all the way around as if it rested on a ball bearing. He held her gaze for a moment before she rounded the stairwell to the sixth floor, out of sight. He was certain he had seen correctly: her neck twisted almost all the way around.

*

That night he slept very little. He stared out his open window at the city lights punctuating the darkness and wondered what was hidden under her veil. He could only guess why the young woman had looked at him that way; she had taken him into her confidence with a look, if only for a moment. It startled him, and he replayed it in his mind.

*

The following two days he had off from work. He normally went to a museum or cycled across the city to the Bois de Boulogne, where he would read in a hidden alcove of conifers and nap as the sun filtered through the branches to warm his face. But he couldn't get the young woman out of his mind. In the shower he moved his head from side to side just to see how far he could twist it, but he did little more than strain his neck and get water in his ears. He dressed and went down the street and got a café au lait from the tabac. His upstairs neighbor was there, and stared at him for some time, before leaving.

He ordered a second coffee because he was tired from going in and out of a restless sleep. Then he left and purchased a baguette from the *boulangerie* and some ham and raw duck from the *boucher* and decided to stay in for the rest of the day. He didn't have the energy to go to the *laverie*, even though his hamper was overflowing. On his way home he saw more women in full head coverings than he had noticed before. He studied them as they passed, and wondered what the women looked like underneath, if all of them could walk forward with their heads facing backward. He couldn't tell, and imagined them quickly looking back at him as he passed, their necks twisted inexplicably backward.

*

Back at his apartment he climbed the stairs slowly and sat in his kitchen at a small round table and ate the baguette dry, without condiment or meat, until the roof of his mouth was shredded. He propped his door open and stared at the empty stairwell for an hour, but no one passed; the building didn't shift and the stairs didn't creak under their own weight. As he drank a 1664, a light stream of air coursed through his apartment, coming in the open window and whooshing out his front door. The building was quiet, and he was eager for the night to come.

Hours passed. He ate muesli with milk and bits of dark chocolate for dinner. The outside light coming through his window dimmed until dusk took the city under its veil and artificial light took its place. The man from upstairs came up the steps and slowed as he walked past the open door. The two men made eye contact for a moment before the short man rounded the stairs and disappeared out of sight. Shortly afterward a small owl landed on the window-sill and seemed to study the arrangement of furniture in the living room: a small futon couch, an old television on a stand wedged in the corner, a wooden coffee table in the middle of the room, and a bookshelf on the back wall sagging under the weight of all the used books he'd purchased from Shakespeare and Company.

An hour later he heard a door open somewhere on the floor above him, but no one came down the stairs. It was after 22:00. He heard the familiar sound of the stairwell skylight opening and then closing. He didn't wait to hear more, and immediately left his apartment, scaling the stairs two at a time until he was at the base of the ladder beyond the landing of the sixth floor, the only point of access for the rooftop. He held on to the narrow railings and thought briefly about surprising whoever was on the roof. He figured if it weren't the young woman from last night it would be an awkward encounter. He let a moment pass. At the top of the ladder he lifted the skylight and poked his head through the opening. He looked the length of the roof in both directions and didn't see anyone, just a small, lone owl gripping the edge of the roof, surveying the neighborhood. He was certain he had heard someone access the roof. He decided to go all the way up. The night air was cool and he walked to the edge, where it slanted down and away from the flat center. There was no one else up there, and if someone had jumped, he couldn't see where they went.

When he turned around a dark figure stood motionless at the other end of the roof. It was the young woman. She was precariously close to the edge, facing away from him, her body locked in place. He studied her from behind, and wondered what she was doing; after a moment she looked back at him quickly, though her body from the shoulders down didn't move. She removed her veil. It took a moment for his eyes to focus, but he was seeing correctly. She had large orange eyes that punched through the dark shadow of her flat facial disc, a tiny hooked bill, and tawny, pointed ear tufts illuminated by the city lights and the moonlight cutting through the cloud cover. She faced him and stepped out of her burqa; his instinct was to turn away, but he didn't. Her arms, legs, and torso were covered in a light down of brindle feathers, a beautiful plumage that camouflaged her breasts and everything underneath.

He took her in. She was beautiful, her black talon-toes gripping the copper gutter. Her eyes glowed. He stood where he was, mouth open, caught in a moment of revelatory disbelief. Then she turned again, showing her mottled tail, and disappeared off the side of the building. He shouted *hey!* but she was gone. She had jumped out and away from the copper gutters. He slowly walked across the roof, careful with his foot placement, to the edge where he saw her jump. He toed toward the edge and looked down. There wasn't a body splattered on the sidewalk below. He looked around in a wide panorama, taking in the city and the unending line of rooftops. He didn't know what to make of any of it. He walked back to the center of the roof and sat down, and massaged his temples. He stayed on the roof hoping she would return. Within a couple of hours he fell asleep, and didn't wake until early morning, when it was still dark. A small owl was staring at him from its perch on one of the nearby chimneys. It didn't blink.

*

That morning he found a note that had been slid under his front door. In uneven script it read: *please leave the roof alone, sir.* It was not signed. He didn't know if the note represented a threat or if it was simply a request from someone on the top floor who was tired of hearing his footfalls on the roof at night. He dressed and went to the *boucherie* and purchased a small amount of foie gras. He thought about the note, and resolved to make his steps lighter. He waited for night to fall, and when it did he went to the rooftop with the raw duck from the day before and the fresh foie gras. He wanted to present it to the young woman as a friendship offering. He knew that owls preyed on ducks and geese in the wild, and it was the most sensible gift he could think to get. Two hours passed before she poked her head through the skylight, and emerged onto the roof. They hadn't spoken before, and he didn't expect that they would. His French was okay, and he didn't know if she was fluent in anything other than Arabic. Her talon-toes clacked on the rooftop as she walked to the center where he was sitting with his legs crossed. She gathered her burqa and lowered herself across from him, and also crossed her legs.

He could tell she was staring at him from behind the mesh screen. After a moment he couldn't hold her gaze and he looked away. For the first time he noticed the buzz of traffic below, scooters loudly accelerating up the hill and dogs barking somewhere in the distance. They sat facing each other for a while, and he tried not to gawk at her exposed feet; up close the black talons glinted under the night sky and he marveled that such a creature existed. He uncovered the duck and the foie gras and offered it to her. She bowed her head in thanks and he placed the meat, still wrapped loosely in paper, at her feet. The raw duck attracted two cautious owls that landed on one of the neighboring television antennas. They kept their distance, but didn't take their eyes off of the meat. She removed her head covering and he felt her orange eyes burn through him; he couldn't look away. Up close her features were even more brilliant.

After finishing most of the duck and all of the foie gras, the young woman stood up and approached the two small owls. She fed them the remainder of the duck, and once it was gone, they returned to their nests at the edge of the roof. She returned to him and did not sit.

"Merci," she said, in a low, almost imperceptible voice. Her bill moved ever so slightly in the middle of her round, plate-like face.

"You're welcome," he said, and looked up at her.

As she had done the night before, she walked to the edge of the roof and stepped out of her burqa. She looked back at him one last time and then disappeared.

*

After working his way down the ladder he was startled to see the young woman's father standing outside of their apartment door. The father had his hands clasped together and he was holding them in front of his stomach, and seemed to know he had been on the roof with his daughter.

"S'il vous plaît laissez ma fille toute seule," the father said. "Elle est allée à pondre ses oeufs, et vous n'aurez pas la voir à nouveau. J'ai honte."

"I'm sorry for bothering her," he said, a bit startled at what the father had said. "I didn't know." He paused. "Where will she lay the eggs?"

"Delà de la ville, dans la forêt," the father said.

"I'm sorry for my intrusion," he said, and noticed the scar on the man's neck again. "I meant no harm."

"Comment pourriez-vous savoir?" the father said, and walked back into his apartment.

*

The next day he had to give the 11:00 bike tour. After he got out of the shower he heard activity coming from the stairwell. When he was dressed he opened the door and saw men in navy-blue shirts carrying boxes down from the sixth floor. The young woman's father came down the stairs after a few minutes, carrying a small wooden box and a new black suitcase.

"Where are you going?" he asked.

The father stopped on the landing.

"Je vais dans la forêt pour être avec elle," the father said.

"Will she come back?" he asked.

"Jamais," the father said, and continued down the stairs.

"Never," he repeated, and stood watching the father round the stairwell until he was out of sight.

The morning was getting away from him and he had to cycle across town. It had been a strange two days. He felt unsettled, as if he weren't supposed to know these things. He walked over to the coffee table where he left his keys and phone, and found a note resting on the edge of the table. Before picking it up he looked out the open window. He could hear and smell the neighborhood outside. He looked at the note once again. She had been here. He pictured the city limits of Paris, and the small towns beyond that shed their pavement for rolling hills, and how all of it bled into overgrown forest. She was somewhere out there. He grabbed his phone off the coffee table and called the bike shop. The office manager answered and he told her he was ill, too sick to lead a tour. He hung up, tucked the note in his back pocket and grabbed his bike. He reasoned he could find the young woman if he tried, and he knew where to start. He first stopped at the *boucherie* and filled his backpack. Then he cycled west, toward the Bois de Boulogne and Forêt de Rouvray. He hoped to find her after nightfall.

Tunneling

He was born slight, two weeks premature. This was Michigan, mid-April 1957. In the minutes following delivery the doctor blanched, refused to cut the boy's umbilical cord, his hands trembling. He burst through the delivery room doors in green cap and gown, in a panic, searching for the ward chaplain. The hospital was rooted in a Pentecostal enclave, a pine-choked town of less than 5,000 people. The doctor directed the chaplain to lay hands on the boy's ringed stomach, to discern what this deformity meant and ask God to heal the boy. But the chaplain refused to look upon the newborn, said he could not lay hands on the boy because he was not made in the image of God. Outside, a light, steady rain persisted.

The doctor, a rigidly capable man in his fifties, paced the small length of the delivery room in an effort to recall his medical schooling, his text books, medical lore, anything to form a grain of understanding: what he saw did not line up with what he knew, what he believed. He was on the verge of hysteria.

The overhead lights in the delivery room were bright white. At an angle, held to the light, grooves defined the boy's belly. His midsection was a slick gelatinous cushion, the skin accordioned like concentric bands ringing his abdomen from waist to collarbone. Everything else about the boy was normal: two arms and two legs, a penis, and a beautiful head with eyes, nose, ears, and a tiny mouth all in their proper place. The doctor and the nurses, every one of them veterans who had worked together on an English airfield during the Second World War, had never seen anything like this boy.

Legs still in the stirrups, the mother's face was white like milled flour. She had lost a pint or more of blood and was faint when her husband implored one of the nurses to cut the umbilical cord. The mother was wheeled out of the room and taken to recovery one floor down. The doctor left, without word, his face buried in his hands. The father stayed and took the boy in his thick logging arms. The boy wailed, drew short of breath, and wailed some more. His birth fluids bloodied the father's flannel shirt and forearms. A sticky mucous—not blood, not amniotic fluid—coated the boy's midsection.

The father held his son delicately and rocked him back and forth. He was a father for the first time at 33, had just missed the war, and refused to let the nurses swaddle the boy, though it was frightfully cold in the room. The father told the nurses he would keep the boy warm. He bent his head to the boy's chest, wanting to see the concentric bands up close, and listen to the boy's heart, each tiny thump a miracle. Eventually, the father allowed the nurse to swaddle the boy, and they joined the mother in her recovery room. That night, only the mother slept.

*

The next day the family was discharged before breakfast. The father wanted to take the boy away, to the family's rolling acreage in the wilds of Michigan's Upper Peninsula, near the Ontario border. It was their summer cottage, inherited after the mother's father had passed away the previous spring. There the father could fish for trout and salmon and hunt deer; he could revive the old victory garden and plant potatoes, onions, radishes, and tomatoes. At the father's request the administrators made no birth record of the boy, nor did the hospital want to lay claim to the boy. The ward chaplain blessed the mop water before the delivery room was cleaned, and everyone involved resolved to keep the secret of the boy's birth, his deformity, fearful of the certain godlessness of the family.

Curbside, the mother sat in a daze in her wheelchair letting the last of the morphine work its way through her sore body. The family was in the rear of the hospital by the ambulatory entrance, out of sight. The nurse who cut the boy's umbilical chord helped the mother into the family's black Hudson Commodore; she had written her address and telephone number on a small piece of paper and handed it to the mother. She said to call if they ever needed anything. The boy, swaddled, squirmed in the mother's arms. The cloth was damp around the stomach, and the mother could feel the power of the muscular contractions in the boy's tiny midsection. She had felt this when the boy was still in her womb.

It took almost three hours to get home, to their cottage on the outskirts of an unincorporated township. The father drove slow and steady northward on the winding two-lane highway. Rows of quaking aspens banded the road on either side. The spring thaw brought with it bright green and blooming vegetation in the woods beyond the road, ringing the great Lake Michigan a half mile west. There was a 45-minute car-ferry across the Straits of Mackinac. In the distance, the Mackinac Bridge, which was set to connect the Upper Peninsula with Lower Michigan, was nearing completion and set to open in November. The father held the boy on the ferry, sheltered him from the wind and also from inquisitive older women. The boy was his greatest joy. He kissed the boy's forehead and looked at the near-complete Mackinac Bridge and regarded it as an unwelcome intrusion. He was taking the boy north, where he would be safe from the outside world.

*

The boy grew fast. His torso was the first to stretch, and the color of his skin faded to dead lavender. In a matter of months the boy was the size of a toddler, and his arms were muscular. The father recognized the family logging genes with pride.

The mother had not yet adjusted to the boy. She had fallen into a thick depression. He wouldn't take to her breast milk and her bosom swelled and cramped, and she would sit in pain at the end of her bed sobbing, milking herself for relief. She kept a leather-bound journal on her nightstand, but only noted the dates at the top of the page as they passed, and could not bring herself to write about the boy.

Most mornings the father found the corners of the boy's mouth crusted with dirt, bits of soil caught in the wispy meringue of hair atop his head. This mystery was solved in early June. Summer had encroached on the acreage, and afternoon sunlight stretched deep into the evening. The wooden cottage sat like a lone Monopoly piece on the property; its wrap-around porch and picture windows looked out at a small patch of open meadow that rolled toward the clear blue water of a glacial lake not forty yards away. The father had just hung a porch swing, had fashioned every bit of it in the wood-shed behind the cottage, back where his father in-law's old maroon Ford F1 pick-up was still garaged. The mother, outside for the first time in days, was coaxed into spreading a picnic quilt. The three of them sat together in the yard, half shaded by the large pine spiking upward out of the soft, fertile ground.

After studying the porch swing from their vantage on the front lawn, the father decided it was tilted ever so slightly to the left and he resolved to raise the left side by one chain-link. The mother was clutching her breasts and looking out toward the lake at three blue herons standing in shallow water. The boy, in nothing but a cloth diaper and a bonnet to shade him from the sun, held his small hands at his sides and slithered off of the patchwork quilt. There was rich loamy soil between the blades of grass and the boy found it and buried his mouth in the dirt and ate. The father bounded off the porch when he saw the boy face down in the grass, worried that the boy was suffocating. The father cried to the mother and his booming voice snapped her from a trance.

The father got to the boy and picked him up in one sweeping motion. There was a slight, rounded depression in the yard where the boy had eaten away the bits of grass and soil. By now the boy was heavy, had been growing without the benefit of breast milk for weeks. Gently, the father placed the boy on the ground, and he began to eat again. Five, ten minutes passed, and the boy created a minor concavity in the lawn, now neck deep. The father studied the boy, and after another minute or so the boy was satisfied and, like a normal baby, crawled back to the quilt. The father had seen the boy move like this before. Sometimes he crawled, and other times he moved quickly on his belly like a snake, or a worm. The father took the boy in his arms and wiped the boy's chin, where wet soil had muddied and streaked his face. You have to watch the boy, the father said. You have to watch him. But the mother didn't regard her husband, paid him no mind. She cradled her chest and walked toward the house, to bed.

*

The father had been taking photographs of the boy with his father in-law's old Polaroid Model 95 from the day of his birth, and now, if he looked at the pictures in quick succession, or flipped through them as if they were a deck of playing cards, he could watch the boy change from one frame to the next, as if he were watching a miniature black and white movie. The father knew how to develop film. He would eagerly come out of a makeshift darkroom in the guest bedroom and add the latest picture and flip through the growing booklet. Sometimes he ruined an exposure and would steam about it for hours. The mother would stay in her bedroom most days, and had no interest in the flip-book, wouldn't look at it when the father brought it in. But the father would show it to the boy in the mornings, and tell the boy that he was going to grow up big and strong like his father.

One night in late August the father took the boy out to the front porch. Neither could sleep, and a curtain of rain was falling. The boy loved the rain, loved to play in the mud and bury his head in the dirt until his mouth grew tired of burrowing. By now shallow holes dotted the meadow around the cottage. Some were rather deep and the boy, now six months old and the size of a six year old, was fast and powerful. He couldn't talk yet, but he made sounds with his mouth and nodded his head yes or no.

After a while, this became routine. The father would take the boy outside and watch him play with the moon reflecting off the lake. Sometimes clouds would roll in and the canopy of trees would hold darkness below their limbs. This would make it hard to find the boy. On nights like this the father would put his head in the cavernous holes and call after the boy until he grew hoarse. Retrieving him could take hours, especially in the rain. The father, harried, would dart from hole to hole slipping in the mud, frantically searching. Then the boy would silently surprise his father and sidle up next to him. The father would yell in his relief, pick up the sodden boy and press him to his chest. Then they would wade out into the lake water, the father clutching the boy, letting the gentle water wash over their soiled bodies.

*

By the following April the boy looked like he was 12. He could talk, he was tall and strong when he walked upright, and the rings from his belly had taken form all over his body. He produced a steady coat of mucous from his pores. The father had built the boy an open-air room in the wood shed so that he could be outside and burrow whenever he pleased. The father would sit on the porch in his swing and watch the boy, and when he couldn't see the boy he would simply listen for him tunneling through the yard, making figure eights around and under the roots of the biggest trees.

One evening, a dry night after days of steady rain, the boy ran from the wood shed and stood before his father on the porch. It was the first time that the two had stood near eye to eye. In the dim porch light the two looked cut from the same stone. The boy hugged his father and they held on to each other for several minutes. The father knew what this meant, and asked if he would see the boy again. The boy nodded, and said that he would, someday. Then the father said, don't break your mother's heart. He couldn't bring himself to tell the boy not to break his own. The boy said he loved him, and dropped to his stomach and slid off the front porch. The boy wriggled from his clothes and disappeared into the first hole he came to, his feet trailing out of sight.

The father sat staring at the hole until the sun came up. It had misted throughout the night and moisture choked the air. By mid-morning the father was asleep in the porch swing. He woke when the mother slammed the trunk of their old Commodore. She said they needed to leave, put this all behind them. The father had the keys in a kitchen drawer. When he opened the drawer he saw a crumpled piece of paper with an address on it. He remembered the nurse and retrieved a sheet of paper from the rolltop desk. The father simply wrote "the boy is gone" in neat cursive. He didn't sign the letter, found an envelope and stamp, and was done with it. In the living room he picked up the photo flipbook, now swollen with more than 300 pictures, and watched his boy grow from a baby into whatever it was he had become. The father's eyes grew glassy. He met his wife by the Commodore. He handed the flipbook and the letter to her, along with the keys, and said he couldn't leave. She didn't protest, and he didn't expect her to. They said goodbye and held each other until he kissed her on the cheek. He imagined his wife driving back over the newly completed Mackinac Bridge toward Traverse City, looking in the rearview mirror at the thick forests of the Upper Peninsula, thinking about the boy, and hoping no one else would ever find him. The thought terrified him.

The Boy and The Bear

The boy woke in the forest, covered in snow, and blinked at the nickel-sized flurries falling on his face. He looked closely at his forearms and hands: dark black hair, brittle as icicles, and claws that shone like dull bone. He lay under the hangover of a jagged stand of rocks near the banks of a river carrying drift ice southward. A large black bear had its snout near the boy's face, its breath warm and wet. Wind blew snow from the shoulders of the tall pines on either side of the river and cracking wood echoed through the forest.

The boy focused on the bear before him and didn't move. The boy was cold, his nose frozen with ice that cleaved as he drew in full, waking breaths. His lungs burned with the deepness of his breathing. The boy couldn't remember how long he had been asleep, hibernating. When he entered the forest months ago, a chill hung in the air and the mountains loomed beyond the balding tree limbs. Now everything was white, bits of brown peeking through at the base of trees and where outsized boulders broke through the powder. The boy had run from his village until he was lost among the pines and small earthen dens that pockmarked the hard packed ground. That was some time ago. His arms and legs had been covered in a soft down of fur then, as if a watercolorist had put the boy on an easel and gone to work detailing every hair.

As he looked at the bear the boy thought of his parents. His mother and father had locked him in the root cellar after his ears grew pointed and his teeth became too long and sharp for his mouth to contain. They said they wouldn't feel safe with a bear living in the house, not after his brother had roared forth from their front door four years before and pawed through the village before being shot near the church, which anchored the village, its white steeple rising skyward to the lightening rod atop the wooden cross. His brother continued toward the thick wood leaving a trail of blood and disappeared into the dense summer foliage.

Four years later, as if overnight, the boy showed signs of changing like his older brother: first a curved back and an inclination to walk on all fours, and then a deep growling voice that sunk low on hard consonants. Finally, in late October, his father manhandled him outside late one evening. All the boy could do was growl and swipe at the air in front of him. They struggled against each other. The father covered the boy's mouth with his hand, which smelled strongly of pork and dirt. His father's arms were round with muscle from working the fields, plowing rows, seeding corn and wheat, wrestling livestock. The boy was not yet big enough to challenge his father and he went quickly into the cellar, worked his way down the mud-speckled steps and looked over his shoulder as his father latched the door shut. He let out a growl that hurt his ears in the small space of the cellar, which held the scent of mildew, dusty corn-husks, and discarded bits of wheat chaff.

The boy watched the village from a slit in the cellar door. Gray smoke billowed from tin-capped chimneys on thatched roofs. Women and girls carried pails of water from a stone-lined well, boys chopped wood, and men led teams of oxen into fields ringing the village, all of them preparing for the cold that would soon grip the valley. The boy's mother chanced a visit once, held her palm to the latch on the cellar door and blocked what light bled through the cracks. The boy heard her whimpering, or she could have been humming a hymn. The lightness of her voice was stolen in the crisp air rushing through the village. The boy cried out to his mother, but by then his voice was deep and startling. She turned quickly, held up the hem of her dress, and rushed to the small house where the boy knew she would prep a stew or pot roast, her delicious bread certainly ready for the oven.

The cellar was cold and damp. The dusting of hair that covered the boy's body kept him warm. When he looked down he saw a snout taking shape in the middle of his face, wet and dark-colored in the dim light. The boy's clothes were tight and the leather of his boots dug into his feet, so painful he had to take them off. It took a week, but the boy used his claws and the tip of his snout to dig out from the cellar. He emerged under the wall abutting the edge of the forest and fled unnoticed in the middle of the night. The boy ran toward the mountains until he was lost and tired, panting like an animal.

With the bear looking over him, the boy rose steadily until he was firmly on all fours. He felt like a statue, his coat of fur matted and frozen; bending his knees felt like breaking through a thin vein of stone. The boy and the bear stood nose to nose, their breath suspended like mist between them. The bear's right ear was half missing and his right eye had the rheumy blue glaze of an old man's cataract. The bear licked the boy's face and then turned to walk along the bank of the river; he occasionally pawed at the thick winter water. The bear had a hitch in his gait, and the boy followed closely behind. They continued into the forest and night fell. The boy followed the bear's tracks under a full moon until they found a home deep in the thick wood, and in time he thought of the village no more.

And Finally The Tragedy

And finally the tragedy. The boy's parents had selected a wooden casket with fine grained eddies streaking its polished sides, ready to be lowered into a family plot when they found him. It wasn't that the boy had been lost and then found dead—that would have been okay. The tragedy was that the boy was found, that he came to, hair matted and sweaty on his forehead. A team of hound dogs with wet salty noses trained on dirty dry field brush found the boy near twilight. The townsfolk were close behind, stabbing lit torches skyward.

The field was blue with moonlight, banded with a stand of trees and a dead creek bed cracked bank to bank. The sounding footfalls of fleeing boar drummed the hardpacked ground. Blackbirds spooked from treetops, feathers shined metallic in flight, and the only thing left in the field was the boy and the townsfolk and the sound of hound dogs panting for water and wind agitating petrified tree branches.

The boy lay in a slight depression of his own making, his chest rising and falling. He had tumbled from the stars, had been swinging satellite to satellite when he fell. We made a ring of silhouettes five or six bodies deep around the boy. When the boy's eyes opened the women hummed hymns and the men nervously worked their calloused hands together. As Reverend, I bent down and looked into his face. His cheeks, where a spray of freckles had been, were now a swirl of galaxies, glowing faint with the matter of the universe. I felt a crush of bodies peering over my shoulders, an expectant congregation. Torches were duffed and the hound dogs bellied to the ground. It was up to me to make sense of the boy, but I found no purchase in what I saw before me. His eyes flickered bright as stars pinpricked in the firmament.

Then the boy opened his mouth, cavernous as a two-story movie theater. I feared he would swallow us whole. Inside his mouth was a projector spinning film. It cast bright yellow light onto the night sky and made a translucent screen of moving images. We pushed our chins upward, as if one body. The reel shone with galaxies blooming like colorful flowers before us. Night became day and day became night and on and on it went. Men grew beards white as chalk that swept the ground and women spun their hair into buns that rose like hives. We lost track of time and the screen slowly dimmed and finally the film stopped spinning. Twilight again. The boy closed his mouth and stood. He started walking through the field toward town, the white church steeple rising over an umbrella of trees. We silently followed in a procession. One by one our bodies turned to dust, salting the wind, and our souls burned in the boy's imagination, forever alight.

Acknowledgments

Thank you to my talented and beautiful wife, artist Danielle Huey Kimzey, for reading these stories repeatedly with a keen eye and a generous spirit. Thank you for always believing in me. I love you with all that I am, Danielle! And thanks to my spirited young daughter, June, who I love with all of my heart, and to my boy, who I can't wait to meet upon his birth.

I want to thank Michelle Latiolais and Ron Carlson; they have drawn out the best in my writing, and are the best literary parents a guy could hope for. And to my friends in the MFA Programs In Writing at UC Irvine, thanks to Brendan Park, Eugenie Montague, Justin Lee, Kat Lewin, and Tagert Ellis, who helped me sharpen these stories. To Peggy Hesketh, thank you for your encouragement and mentorship. I'd also like to thank Elizabeth George and the Elizabeth George Foundation for their generous support of my writing.

I'd like to also thank Ramona Ausubel, Roxane Gay, Matt Bell, Kyle Minor, Gabe Durham, Austin Ratner, Harriet Alida Lye, and Josh Woods for taking the time to read this book ahead of its publication and support it with their wonderful words. Thank y'all!

To the editors who first published these stories—Masie Cochran at *Tin House*, Roxane Gay at *PANK*, Gabe Durham at *Dark Sky Magazine*, Harriet Alida Lye at *Her Royal Majesty*, Kim Winternheimer at *The Masters Review*, and Euan Monaghan at *Structo Magazine*—thank you for giving these stories a home. I'm so proud to be part of your literary families!

I want to give a heartfelt thanks to amazing artist Pat Perry for his generosity and allowing me to use "Free Soil Thirty-One" for the cover image. I love Pat's work, and I'm honored he agreed to be part of this book.

Special thanks to Diane Goettel, Kit Frick, and the rest of the Black Lawrence Press team for loving this book, for confidently putting it into the world, and for selecting this collection of six short stories for the Black River Chapbook Competition.

Finally, thanks to my family for always cheering me on, especially my father, Jackie Kimzey. Pops, you're just the best father a son could hope to have. To Russ, Brian, and Luke, I couldn't do life without the three of you, my brothers, my best friends. Thank you for your love and support. And to my mother, Connie, who I know is so proud of me. I miss you, mom, and I love you dearly! And to Michelle, who has always encouraged me!

Thank you all for supporting this book. I can't thank you enough!

Photo: Danielle Huey Kimzey

Blake Kimzey grew up in small-town Texas. He is a graduate of the MFA Programs In Writing at UC Irvine. Blake is the recipient of a generous 2013 Emerging Writer Grant from The Elizabeth George Foundation. His work has been broadcast on NPR and published by *Tin House*, *FiveChapters*, *Puerto del Sol*, *The Los Angeles Review*, *Short Fiction*, *Mid-American Review*, *The Lifted Brow*, *PANK*, *Juked*, *Keyhole*, *Monkeybicycle*, and *Surreal South '13*, among others. Blake is currently writing his first novel, and lives in Dallas with his wife and two children.